The whisper of a fairy
The magic of its word
Will help those in the forest
Whenever it is heard

And when there is danger
Wherever there is need
A fairy's care and help
Will be there indeed

a min*e*dition book
published by Penguin Young Readers Group

Manufactured in Hong Kong by Wide World Ltd.
Typesetting in Frutiger, by Adrian Frutiger.
Color separation by Fotoriproduzione Grafiche, Verona, Italy.

Library of Congress Cataloging-in-Publication Data available upon request.

ISBN 978-0-698-40070-2

10 9 8 7 6 5 4 3 2 1
First Impression

For more information please visit our website: www.minedition.com

Also published in this series:

Amar, the Earth Fairy
Runya, the Fire Fairy
Tara, the Air Fairy

Aelin, the Water Fairy

by Simone Lindner
Illustrated by Christa Unzner
Translated by Kathryn Bishop

minedition

One bright night when the moon was full, Aelin, the
Water Fairy, sat combing her long hair. She could see
her reflection in the water of the spring, swirling
around her feet.
Suddenly she saw something under the water's surface.
First there was a little head, then two legs, and finally,
a dark shell emerged.
It was Nara the turtle.
Aelin laughed and helped her friend up onto the rock.

"Aelin," said the little turtle, completely out of breath.
"You have to come, please. We need your help!
The water from the spring isn't flowing to the lake any-
more, and it's drying out. There is only a little pool left.
It's terrible! The plants are dry, the fish don't have
enough room to swim, and there is not enough water
for the animals to drink!"

"How could this happen?" wondered Aelin. "It's too dark now, I'm afraid. We'll leave first thing in the morning." The Water Fairy made a soft bed of moss for them to sleep on, and they slept until the first birds woke them in the morning.

"I'll fly to the lake and see what's happened,"
announced Aelin. "Nara, you should follow the water
to the point where it stops and wait for me there."

Aelin lifted up into the air and soon Nara could only see
a whirling spot that quickly disappeared between the trees.
Then the turtle was off, swimming the course of the water.

Aelin was shocked. Where once the lake had been, there was now just a murky little pool. And the plants along the edge hung their thirsty heads.

Aelin dove into the water, looking for Grandfather Lim, the old carp. Finally, she saw him swimming in the middle of a swarm of fish.

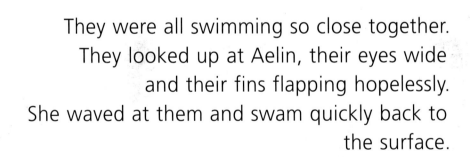

They were all swimming so close together. They looked up at Aelin, their eyes wide and their fins flapping hopelessly. She waved at them and swam quickly back to the surface.

"There is not enough water for them," she whispered. "I'll help you! Don't worry!" she called back.

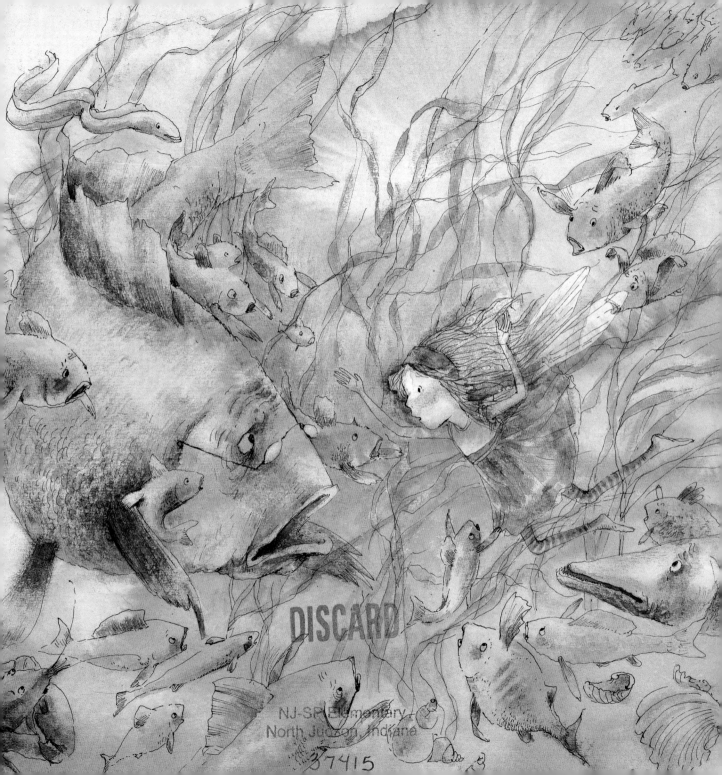

Aelin took off again, flying close to the water, toward the spring. Only a tiny stream of water was able to make its way through the sand into the lake. She watched carefully as she flew, until she discovered the problem.

A giant tree was lying across the stream, blocking the water's path. Branches and leaves had collected, creating a dam. No water could flow through.

"See what that giant log has done?"
said Nara, who was waiting for Aelin.
The thick trunk of the tree had been gnawed through,
and it had fallen into the stream.
"This is the work of the beaver," said Aelin. "If he was
able to get it into the water, he should be able to help
get it out. I'll go and find him."

"Oh no," mumbled the beaver, shaking his head when he saw what had happened. "This is not what I wanted!"

"Fussing isn't the answer," said Aelin. "Everyone must help. We have to push the tree."

So the fairy, the beaver, the turtle, and a few frogs began to push. But nothing happened. It wouldn't budge an inch.

The little fairy sat down on the log to think. Everyone was quiet. Only the beaver was restless, running back and forth, shaking his head, muttering, "This is not what I wanted! This is not what I wanted at all."

Softly Aelin started singing a tune from the world of magical beings, and then she called out...

Ni nalla tulu !
I call for help!

Heart of a fairy, brave and true
Show me now what I must do
Give me an answer, help me to know
How I can make this water flow

"I've got it!" she shouted.
"We need to break through the dam
from underneath," she said. "Come
everyone, help me, please!"

And so they started pulling the first branches from the dam.
Other water creatures came to help too.
A crab started snipping away at some twigs. Nara,
the forest mice, and a wild duck carried all the branches
away. The frogs rolled the stones away, and the fish
fanned their fins, clearing out the leaves. The beaver
gnawed furiously, and soon the log was very thin in
the middle.

Aelin felt a strong pull in the water, and then the dam
broke with a loud rumble. The water crashed down
its dried-out course. Aelin and all the animals
swam with the current. It was like a water slide
taking them all the way back to the lake.
Everyone would be safe now that the water
was flowing in.

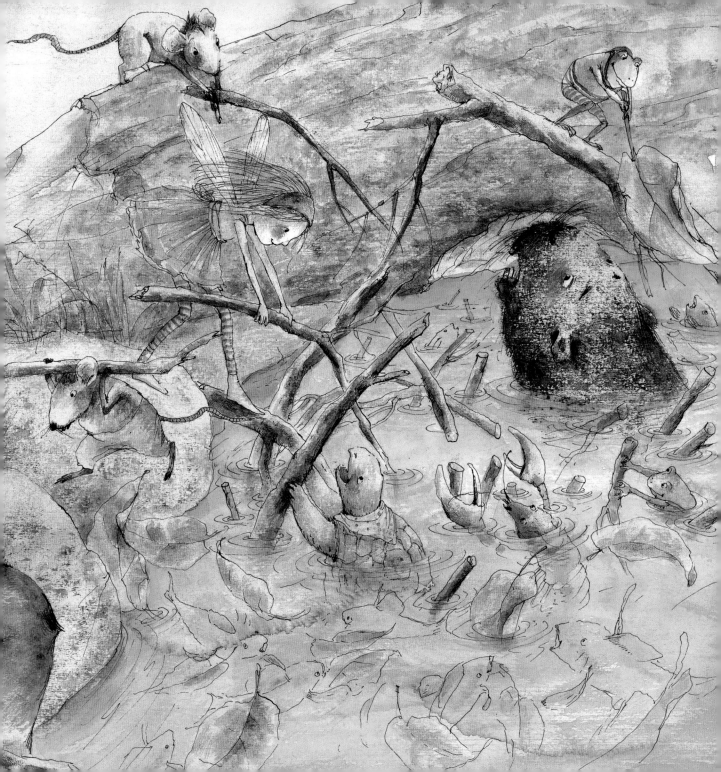

The little Water Fairy dove down as Grandfather Lim,
the old carp, was swimming happily toward her.
She held his fins tightly, and they whirled around and around.
The fish danced with them, too.
Aelin swam back to the surface and sat down on the leaf of a
water lily to rest. She was humming a little song when
something started to twinkle in the sky. A bright light appeared,
and then a gentle voice said,
"Aelin, Water Fairy, you have done your work well."

"*Bereth*, the Fairy Queen," whispered Aelin respectfully as she
curtsied.
The Queen glistened in her flowing white dress, sparkling with
the light of a thousand diamonds. Her long hair shone, and her
delicate wings shimmered with every color of the rainbow.

"Aelin, you are a very special Water Fairy,"
said the Queen. "For a long time you have cared
for the water, the plants, and the animals.
I would now like to send you into the world of
human children. Are you ready to go?"

Aelin looked surprised. Then her face lit up
and she nodded happily.

The Queen opened a shiny little shell and took out
a gold ring.
"Aelin, Water Fairy, I hereby present to you the
magic fairy ring, the ring of your element, water."

"The ring will serve you in the human world. It will help you exchange secret messages, and it will seal your friendships. When it is placed on the ground it will create a large circle, and only those who enter it will be able to see you, to speak and dance with you.

From now on you are to be a friend and protector of a human child. That child is reading this story and is waiting for you."

Aelin beamed and placed the ring on her finger.

Then the shining light disappeared as suddenly as it had come.
For Aelin, the Water Fairy, a new adventure was about to begin…

Could her adventure
be with *you?*

Which of the elements suits you best?

WATER and *Aelin*

1. imaginative
2. bubbly
3. creative
4. pure
5. lakes, rivers
6. sea, ocean
7. waves
8. waterfalls
9. raindrops, snowflakes
10. ice crystals
11. slide, float
12. swim

FIRE and *Runya*

1. fiery
2. warm-hearted
3. explosive
4. enthusiastic
5. full of energy
6. gives warmth
7. brings light in the darkness
8. sparkling
9. crackle
10. sun
11. fire light
12. firesides

EARTH and *Amar* ○

1. rascal
2. steadfast
3. healing abilities
4. good-natured
5. rocks and stones
6. mountains and valley
7. forests and meadows
8. earth, trees, and roots
9. plants and flowers
10. digging
11. playing in the sand
12. all 4 seasons

Air and *Tara*

1. happy
2. playful
3. quick-tempered
4. wind
5. storm
6. sky
7. clouds
8. flying with birds
9. soaring, floating
10. feeling free as a breeze
11. feeling light as a feather
12. pinwheels and kites

When you have finished the book and have discovered the wonders of the fairy, open this letter. It was written especially for you!